Also by Barbara O'Connor

FAME AND GLORY
IN FREEDOM, GEORGIA

FAME AND GLORY
IN FREEDOM, GEORGIA

BARBARA O'CONNOR

SQUARE
FISH

Farrar Straus Giroux

SQUARE FISH

An Imprint of Macmillan

FAME AND GLORY IN FREEDOM, GEORGIA.
Copyright © 2003 by Barbara O'Connor.
All rights reserved. Printed in the United States of America by
R. R. Donnelley & Sons Company, Harrisonburg, Virginia.
For information, address Square Fish, 175 Fifth Avenue, New York, NY 10010.

Square Fish and the Square Fish logo are trademarks of Macmillan and
are used by Farrar Straus Giroux under license from Macmillan.

Library of Congress Cataloging-in-Publication Data
O'Connor, Barbara.
    Fame and glory in Freedom, Georgia / Barbara O'Connor.
        p.   cm.
    Summary: Unpopular sixth-grader Burdette "Bird" Weaver persuades the new
boy at school, who everyone thinks is mean and dumb, to be her partner for a
spelling bee that might win her everything she's ever wanted.
    ISBN 978-0-374-40018-7
    [1. Interpersonal relations—Fiction. 2. Schools—Fiction. 3. Contests—Fiction.
4. Popularity—Fiction.] I. Title.
PZ7.O217 Fam 2003   [Fic]—dc21   2002190212

Originally published in the United States by Farrar Straus Giroux
First Square Fish Edition: February 2012
Square Fish logo designed by Filomena Tuosto
mackids.com

10 9 8 7 6

AR: 4.3 / LEXILE: 740L

To Barbara Markowitz,
agent and friend

This one's for you

FAME AND GLORY
in FREEDOM, GEORGIA

Harlem Tate hadn't been in Freedom, Georgia, more than three days before it was clear that nobody wanted anything to do with him. Nobody except me, that is. I had a burning desire to be his friend.

All everybody else saw in him was a silent, glaring kid who didn't smell too good. Me? I could tell by his scowling face that Harlem Tate didn't get many chances to see the good in folks. Like me. And something about his hunched-over way of walking told me Harlem Tate's insides were churning up with needing something. Like mine.

So when I sat on Miss Delphine Reese's front porch going over my day like I always do, I told her my plan.

"He's gonna be my friend," I said, watching her pick dead leaves off the potted plants.

"Is he now?" Miss Delphine stuffed the leaves in the pocket of her jeans and smiled at me.

"Well, maybe." I propped my feet up on the railing in front of me and frowned at my legs, all skinny and bruised up. How come I couldn't have legs like Celia Pruitt or Charlene Stokeley? Maybe I could sit with them at lunch if my legs weren't so ugly.

I told Miss Delphine everything I knew about Harlem. How he came here from Valdosta to live with Mr. Moody. How he's taller than anybody in sixth grade and even taller than lots of the eighth graders. I told her how he has this hunched-over way of walking and how he glares all the time and how everybody thinks he looks mean and acts dumb.

"He sits way in the back of the class and if Mrs. Moore asks him something, half the time he don't even answer," I said. "Brian Sutter said he's been in the sixth grade for three years."

Miss Delphine pressed her lips together in that way that makes her dimples show.

"Aw, phooey." She flapped her hand at me. "I wouldn't listen to talk like that," she said.

"Harlem *is* tall," I said. "You should see him."

Miss Delphine clicked her Passion Pink fingernails on the arm of her chair while I told her more stuff.

"Everybody at school says he's living with Mr. Moody because his daddy's in prison and his mama choked on a chicken bone at the Holiday Inn," I said.

Miss Delphine smiled and combed her fingers through her fluffy red hair. "Sounds like he could *use* a friend."

Anybody else might have had something more to say about a boy showing up out of nowhere to stay with a crazy old man who chews tobacco and lives over a tattoo parlor and looks for cans on the side of the road. Anybody else might have said if Harlem looks so mean and acts so dumb, then why in the world do I want to go and be his friend? But not Miss Delphine. She's beautiful inside and out. She treats everybody like they have worth—even those worthless kids at school who treat me like dirt for no good reason. And she has a talent for finding the good in everybody—and, believe me, that's hard to do in this town. Some folks in Freedom are so mean in spirit they don't deserve anything better than a good kick. But Miss Delphine, she can look right through their mean spirit and find something the rest of us overlooked.

So I told her some more about my plan. "Nobody else wants to be his friend, see, so that means he's available for me," I said. "I think it was kind of a stroke of luck, don't you? Him coming to Freedom and not having any friends and all?"

She nodded. "A stroke of luck, for sure."

"I took one look at him and I said to myself, 'Bird, here's your chance. Make friends with that kid,' I said, 'before somebody poisons his mind with lies about you.' "

Miss Delphine arched her eyebrows. "Now, who's gonna go and do a thing like that?"

I frowned at my ugly legs again. "Shoot, we'd be here

all day if I start naming 'em all." I licked my finger and wiped dirt off my knee.

She put her hand on top of my hand and squeezed. Her skin was pure white. Not even one little freckle.

A bell jingled from inside the house.

Miss Delphine stood up and ruffled my hair. "I'll be right back," she said.

The screen door slammed behind her. I could hear her voice from the back bedroom and then the hoarse grumble of Pop Reese. I wrinkled my nose just thinking about that old man laying back there in the bed, all teary-eyed and drooling.

Sometimes I feel selfish being so glad that Miss Delphine had to leave her fancy job in Atlanta after her daddy had a stroke. Lucky for me her goodness is so big that she didn't bat an eye when her sister, Alma, told her she better come home and take care of Pop. She just packed her things and came on back to live next door to me again. Mama is all the time telling me to stop pestering Miss Delphine. But I can't help it. There's not much of anything I'd rather do than visit Miss Delphine. Besides, she seems like she don't mind being pestered.

While I waited on her porch, I could hear her bustling around inside, talking real sweet to Pop. Then she came out and sat beside me on the porch again. She smelled like medicine. Her blue eye shadow glittered in the late afternoon sun. I wish my mama would let me wear glittery blue eye shadow like that.

"I love those boots," Miss Delphine said.

I looked down at my dirty white boots. They had been my sister Colleen's marching band boots. I love them 'cause they're so soft and broken in. I was glad Miss Delphine loved them, too.

"Celia Pruitt said they're loser boots," I said. "But I saw Harlem looking at 'em. I could tell he liked 'em."

Miss Delphine smiled and gazed out at the magnolia tree in the front yard. Its leathery leaves spread out across the ground like a giant tepee.

"I remember when Pop planted that tree," Miss Delphine said. "Just look at it now, all grown up and fine as can be." She patted my knee. "Just like Bird," she added.

I grinned and felt my insides swell up with love for Miss Delphine, who always makes me feel good about myself.

"So what do you think about my plan?" I said. "For Harlem Tate to be my friend."

She cocked her head at me and winked. "I think it's a good plan."

"Okay, then, I'll do it. Starting tomorrow, Harlem Tate is gonna be my friend."

I nodded my head real big and sure, like I had confidence. Like my plan was good. Like Harlem Tate really was going to be my friend. But I was glad Miss Delphine couldn't see what was on the inside of me, 'cause inside, I wasn't too sure at all.

When I walked into the cafeteria, Janice Carpenter said real loud, "Red and yellow don't go together, Bird."

I looked down at my red sweater and my yellow shirt and I knew she was right. They looked ugly together. Shoot, I thought. They had looked good this morning when I put them on, but now they didn't.

I pretended like I didn't see those girls poking each other and carrying on. I got my tray and sat way down at the empty end of the table. All around me, kids were smooshing their mashed potatoes flat and flicking their peas. I felt a pea hit me, but I pretended like I didn't notice.

And then I saw Harlem. He was easy to spot 'cause he towered over everybody else. His hair was long, hanging down the back of his neck and covering up his ears. He stood there all hunched over, with his arms dangling clear to his knees. He had a crumpled-up grocery bag in one hand and two cartons of milk in the other.

I waved my arms. "Hey, Harlem! Over here."

He glared in my direction. Some boy shoved him towards my table and then ran off.

I patted the bench beside me. "Sit here," I said.

He sat at the table behind me. I turned around and put my blueberry muffin in front of him. He acted like he didn't even see it.

I kept looking over my shoulder while I ate, keeping an eye on Harlem. I couldn't hardly believe it when he reached in his bag and took out a soggy-looking sandwich wrapped in a page from a magazine. Just whipped that magazine-wrapped sandwich out in front of everybody, like it was normal as anything. Naturally, when the boys at his table got a load of that, they were all laughing and poking and saying how Harlem sure was stupid and maybe he could get some brains tattooed on his head at the tattoo parlor. Stuff like that. When Harlem glared their way they hushed up fast.

Harlem sat there chewing his sandwich, with his hair hanging down in his face. Then somebody told him my blueberry muffin had cooties and if he ate it he was liable to puke. I watched his face, and guess what? He shot me a look. Something about that look gave me a glimmer of hope. Something about that look said, "I been where you been."

So I counted that as a sign, and that afternoon I told Miss Delphine.

"Don't you think that was a sign?" I said.

Miss Delphine was peeling apples. She let the shiny red skins fall onto newspaper spread out on the floor. "Could be," she said. "Did he eat the blueberry muffin?"

"No, but you know what?"

"What?"

"He wrapped it up in that magazine page and took it with him."

Miss Delphine wagged her peeling knife at me. "Now, *that* was a sign," she said. "Why don't you go on over to Mr. Moody's and say hey?"

I shook my head. "Too soon." I took an apple from the stack in front of Miss Delphine and tossed it from hand to hand. "I don't wanna scare him off."

Miss Delphine nodded. "Good thinking."

"Maybe I should give him a present." I chewed on the end of my ponytail. Then I twisted the apple round and round while I held the stem, reciting the alphabet in my head, hoping like anything that stem would break off when I got to "H" (which would be a sign that Harlem would be my friend). It broke off at "E."

Miss Delphine's gold bracelets clanged together as she peeled the apples. "How about an apple pie?" she said.

I shook my head. "Naw. I was thinking something like a T-shirt or a wallet or something."

"Bird." Miss Delphine stopped peeling and leaned towards me. "The way to a man's heart is through his stomach." She licked her fingers, then winked at me. "Trust me, I know."

So that's how it happened that me and Miss Delphine were walking up Augusta Street, carrying an apple pie. Miss Delphine's shoes click-clacked on the sidewalk and her dangly earrings sparkled in the sun like diamonds. I thought she looked like a princess. No, a queen. She looked just like a queen. I don't reckon I'll ever hold a candle to the likes of Miss Delphine. Me with my mousy ole hair and drab ole eyes and bony all over.

"You think Harlem's gonna like this pie?" I said, breathing in a whiff of sweet cinnamon smell.

Miss Delphine put her arm around me. "Sure he is. And he's gonna like you, too."

When we got to the tattoo parlor, we stopped to admire the sign. ELITE TATTOOS. GEORGIA'S FINEST BODY ART. SAFE AND SANITARY. CUSTOM DESIGNS ON REQUEST. Taped on a poster inside the window were pictures of arms and legs and chests and backs, all decorated with dragons, hearts, daggers, and American flags.

I'd walked by this tattoo parlor a million times in my life and had always wanted to go inside. And now I was about to. Me, Miss Delphine, and that apple pie. My stomach was flip-flopping like crazy.

When we opened the door, a bell tinkled.

"Hello," Miss Delphine called out in a singsongy voice.

We waited. No answer. I looked around. It was kind of disappointing in there. A counter with pictures of tattoo designs under the glass top. A couple of folding chairs. Some stools. A cardboard box filled with magazines. A rickety card table covered with paper cups and chewing gum wrappers.

A curtain hung over a door behind the counter. Next to that, stairs led up to the second floor.

"I bet Mr. Moody's place is up there," I said.

Miss Delphine looked up the stairs and called again. "Hellooooo."

Something bumped and scraped across the floor overhead. We both looked up. Muffled voices drifted down the stairs. A door closed.

Then that nasty old Mr. Moody came down the stairs and squinted at us.

"Yeah?" he said. His hair stuck up every which way and his eyes looked all wild. He didn't have on a shirt. His chest was sunken in and covered with wiry gray hairs.

I held the pie up.

"I brought this," I said.

His eyes jerked towards the pie, then to me, then to Miss Delphine, then back to me.

"I don't know you," he said.

"I'm Burdette," I said, still holding up the pie. "But everybody calls me Bird." I grinned and added, "I spell it with an 'I' 'cause 'B-u-r-d' looks stupid, don't you think?"

I tried not to look at the brown tobacco stain worming its way down his chin.

Miss Delphine thrust her hand out at Mr. Moody. "I'm Delphine Reese," she said, smiling her big smile and making her dimples show. "I bet you know my daddy, Jimmy Reese. He was married to Sue Badgers? You remember her. Her daddy owned the car wash over on Macon Highway. Roy Badgers? I bet you remember him."

Mr. Moody squinted at Miss Delphine, then scratched his nasty old chest.

All I could think about right then and there was how in the world Harlem could stand living in this place with that old man. And just as I was thinking that, Harlem came down the stairs, took one look at me and Miss Delphine, and hightailed it right back upstairs.

"Harlem, wait," I called. "I brought you this."

A door slammed and I looked at Miss Delphine, knowing she would know just the right thing to do.

She took the pie from me and held it towards Mr. Moody.

"Bird is all the time thinking about others," she said. "She figured since you have a growing boy here now, you could use this."

"I got sugar diabetes," Mr. Moody snapped like we should've known. He said it loud and exaggerated. "Die-BEE-teez." Like that.

"Then Harlem can have it all," I said, proud of myself for thinking so fast. "You want me to take it up there to him?"

Mr. Moody jerked his head towards the top of the stairs. "Looks like he don't want company," he said.

I looked at Miss Delphine and she looked at me, and before we could get our wits about us, Mr. Moody had disappeared up the stairs.

I turned to Miss Delphine. "I guess my plan didn't work," I said.

She nodded. "Something tells me that boy is gonna be a tough nut to crack."

"Yeah."

"You got to have a backup plan."

"A backup plan," I echoed, looking down at the apple pie in Miss Delphine's hands. "Yeah, I got to have a backup plan."

We walked home in silence, Miss Delphine's shoes click-clacking on the sidewalk and me thinking hard about my backup plan.

All my thoughts about a backup plan went right out the window the next day when I found out about the spelling bee. Mrs. Moore told us about it in this real excited way, but at first I figured it was no big deal. Just another one of those ideas teachers come up with to get kids to study. But the more she talked, the more excited everybody got, and pretty soon a little seed of a thought started growing in my brain. Then we got these papers telling more stuff about the spelling bee, and by the time my eyes got to the bottom of that page, I knew that this was my chance.

All my life, I've had two goals. Two things I want more than anything. One is to get noticed in this town. To make those pea-flicking kids stop and take a look at Burdette Weaver and really see me instead of looking right through me like I'm Casper the Ghost. I don't need anything big-time. Just one short day of fame and glory in Freedom, Georgia, would be fine with me. Shoot, just a couple of minutes of fame and glory would be fine with me. Just enough to show folks my true self that they been missing all these years.

My other goal in life is to get to Disney World. Just once.

So when I read the notice about that spelling bee, I saw right away that here was my ticket to fame and glory and Disney World. Here's why:

First off, it was a sure thing that whoever won that spelling bee would be the center of attention for at least a day. Teachers would be carrying on and all the dumb kids would think you were something and all the smart kids would sit up and take notice of someone smarter than them (but ha, ha, ha is what I was thinking about that).

But besides all that fame and glory that was sure to be heaped on the winner, there were prizes. When I read the list, my legs felt like they wanted to dance a jig right there in the middle of Mrs. Moore's sixth-grade class. Here were the prizes:

Third Place: A world atlas (like anybody would want that!) and two free passes to the movies at the Cineplex on Highway 29.

Second Place: A $15 gift certificate to Record Town in the mall over in Macon; a free round of miniature golf at Starland; and a backpack.

Of course, first place got the best prizes. All kinds of

businesses in Freedom had donated stuff, and the spelling bee winner got to choose three things. Here were some of the choices: a fourteen-karat gold necklace; a three-speed bicycle; four free haircuts; a gift certificate to Bi-Lo grocery store; one month of karate lessons; two months of ballet lessons; two free guitar lessons; a fifteen-volume set of encyclopedias; a free dental exam (like anybody would choose that!); a portable CD player; a Sears clock radio with numbers that shine up on the ceiling; and about ten more things I can't even think of now.

Those prizes were nice and I couldn't help but start planning which three I would choose. But it wasn't until I got to the very bottom of that paper that my heart felt like it had just up and stopped. Here's what it said:

The winner of the Freedom Middle School Spelling Bee will be eligible to compete in the Georgia State Spelling Bee in Atlanta. The lucky winner of the state spelling bee will be treated to a trip to Disney World.

That's right—Disney World. So now you can see why that spelling bee was the ticket to my two goals in life: fame and glory, and Disney World.

I couldn't hardly get my legs to run fast enough to Miss Delphine's that day.

4

Miss Delphine shook her head and whistled. "Those are some real nice prizes," she said.

I twirled my ponytail and stared down at the spelling bee paper in my lap. I had read that list of prizes about a million times.

"I sure would like to win," I said.

"Then do it." Miss Delphine pulled her sweater closed and tucked her feet up under the crocheted afghan on her lap.

"Yeah, right." I rolled my eyes. "Like I got a chance."

Miss Delphine lowered her head and looked at me through her long, fluttery eyelashes. "Well, you don't have a chance if you don't try, right?"

I shrugged.

"Right?" she said again, poking me with one of her long fingernails.

"I suppose."

Miss Delphine's eyebrows shot up and her lips squeezed together. The setting sun behind her made her red hair shimmer with streaks of gold.

"Which prize would you pick?" she said, nodding towards the paper in my lap. "Me, I'd go for that necklace."

I cocked my head like I was thinking, but the truth of the matter was I had only one prize on my mind. Disney World. But (a) I'd never shared my Disney World dream with Miss Delphine before and now I felt silly doing it, and (b) I didn't have one little smidgen of a chance of winning that prize, so what was the use in talking about it anyway. But when I looked up at Miss Delphine with her red-gold hair shimmering around her face and her eyes watching me with hope and expectation, I didn't want to disappoint her. So I said, "Maybe that bike."

But I knew my voice didn't sound too much like a spelling bee winner.

"You *are* going to sign up for that spelling bee, aren't you?" Miss Delphine said.

"Maybe." I looked at my feet, at the rocking chair, at Miss Delphine's turquoise sweater with the silver beads —anywhere but at her face.

She pushed the afghan aside and came over to me. I smelled her talcum powder and I knew I was about to feel better about myself.

"You can do this, Bird," she said, real soft. "I know you

can. Sure, you might not win. But you'll be in there try-ing. It's for certain you won't win if you don't even try." She paused a minute and then added, "Right?"

I thunked the chair with my heels and scratched a mosquito bite on my arm. "I guess."

Miss Delphine stood up and jammed her fists into her waist. "Burdette Weaver," was all she said.

"I'm not such a good speller," I said, my voice coming out shaky and squeaky-like.

"Then you'll have to study, won't you?"

Miss Delphine yanked the screen door open and disap-peared inside. Then she marched back out and dropped a big, heavy book in my lap. *Oxford American Dictionary.*

"There," she said.

It wasn't too often I got irritated at Miss Delphine, but this was definitely cause for irritation.

"How am I going to study every word in here?" I said.

"Start with 'A' and work your way to 'Z,' I reckon."

A bell jingled from inside and Miss Delphine said, "I got to go. You take that book home, okay?"

Then she turned and went inside.

That night, I put the dictionary under my bed so Colleen wouldn't stick her nosy self into my business. I laid in bed and looked up at the ceiling and thought real hard about the spelling bee and Disney World and me. I closed my eyes and saw myself wearing that necklace and riding that bike to karate class. From there, I moved right on along to picturing me riding those spinning teacups at Disney World.

I woke up the next day still clinging to my fantasy. And then I went to school and got whopped upside the head with a big fat dose of reality.

5

Mrs. Moore told us more about the spelling bee and then she said one word that smacked me hard. "Partner." We had to have a partner in the spelling bee.

Well, that was that, I said to myself. I could kiss that spelling bee goodbye. Who was going to be *my* partner? So while Mrs. Moore went on and on about two heads being better than one and blah blah blah, I slumped down in my seat and scribbled on my science notebook.

By lunchtime, it seemed like the whole world had turned into one big Noah's ark. Two by two. Everybody all paired up except the losers. Well, so what? I didn't even care about that spelling bee anyway. Charlene Stokeley could ride her new bike over to Celia Pruitt's house and they could sit there and read their encyclopedias together. Then they could have a sleepover and stare up at the ceiling and see the time up there, shining like starlight from their Sears clock radio.

That afternoon, I walked slow to Miss Delphine's, running my hand along the chain-link fences and kicking acorns off the sidewalk. My feet felt like cement blocks when I climbed the porch steps and knocked on Miss Delphine's door.

"It's open," she hollered from inside.

The screen door squeaked and then slammed shut with a bang behind me.

Miss Delphine sat in her favorite beat-up old chair, working on her cross-stitch. When I told her I wasn't going to be in the spelling bee, she took her pearly reading glasses off and dropped her cross-stitch in her lap.

"How come?"

" 'Cause it's stupid," I said.

"Okay," she said.

She put her glasses back on and went to work on her cross-stitch again, squinting down at the cloth with her tongue poking against the inside of her cheek. She pushed the needle through the cloth with her pinkie finger sticking up in the air like Queen Elizabeth drinking tea.

"So, what's going on with that Harlem boy?" she said.

I was grateful she had changed the subject, but the spelling bee still hovered in the air between us like a spiderweb.

"I can't think of a backup plan," I said.

"You try talking to him?"

"I don't ever get a chance," I said. "He won't sit with

★ 23

me at lunch. And if I wave at him in the hall or something, he acts like he don't even see me."

Miss Delphine raised her arm as she pulled the glossy thread through the cloth. She chuckled and said, "I like that in a man. That's the kind I always go for, too. The kind that make like they don't want nothing to do with you." She leaned forward and winked. "Adds to the fun, don't you think?"

I shook my head. "Harlem doesn't want nothing to do with me or anybody else. I give up trying to be his friend."

Uh-oh. I wished I hadn't said that. Miss Delphine whipped her glasses off, squeezed her mouth up tight, and narrowed her eyes at me.

"Well, you're just in a giving-up mood today, aren't you?" she said.

"No."

"Yes, you are."

"I am not."

"Okay." Then she picked up her cross-stitch and started working again, but I knew she had more words tumbling around inside her 'cause she forgot to put her glasses back on.

"You don't understand," I said. "That boy is weird. He looks like a big ole giant and he's got this long, greasy hair hanging down in his face and anybody so much as blinks at him and he's glaring at 'em mean as anything."

"So?"

"So, who'd want to be his friend anyway?"

"You did, not two days ago."

"Well, I changed my mind." I flicked a fly off my knee and watched it land on the lampshade beside Miss Delphine. I could feel her looking at me. "Something wrong with that?" I snapped.

I wished I could take those angry words back but I couldn't. They hung there between us, all tangled up in that spelling bee spiderweb, so the air in the room was thick with bad feelings.

And now you'll know why I love Miss Delphine when I tell you that she set her cross-stitch aside and waded through that thick air over to where I sat. She knelt down in front of me with her hands on my knees and her powdery smell drifting up at me and she said, "That Harlem boy sure has a treat in store for him when you think of a backup plan and make him your friend."

Now, who wouldn't love a person that says a thing like that?

6

On Saturday, Mama was taking Colleen to get a perm and I had to go with them. I wanted to stay home with Daddy, but he had to sleep before he drove his truck up to Tennessee. I've been told about a million times that driving an eighteen-wheeler takes a rested mind and body, but sometimes it seems like all I ever see of my daddy is when he's snoring on the couch or waving good-bye.

When we got to town, I figured I'd go over to Mrs. Eula Thatcher's Have-to-Have-It Shop and see if anything good came in. Friday is drop-off day, when Mrs. Thatcher lets folks drop off stuff they want to sell.

I love poking around that store. You're liable to find anything in there. I've gotten some good stuff real cheap. Boxing gloves, a light-up globe, a pocket calculator.

So while Mama and Colleen were at the beauty parlor,

I ambled in the direction of the Have-to-Have-It Shop. It was nearly Halloween, but the air was hot and thick, almost like summer. I pushed my bangs off my forehead, wishing I hadn't worn my sweatshirt. And then a funny thing happened. I had my mind set on the Have-to-Have-It Shop, but my feet took me right past it to Elite Tattoos, instead. Just marched me right up to the window and then stopped.

I cupped my hands around my eyes and put my face against the glass. Ray Davis was in there, smoking cigarettes and drinking soda. Ray is the owner of Elite Tattoos. He calls himself a skin artist. The sign on the door says so. RAY DAVIS, SKIN ARTIST.

He looked up.

I waved.

He waved back and took a big puff on his cigarette. And then guess what? Harlem came down the stairs and perched hisself on a stool. He picked up a blue marker and hunched over a big piece of paper on the counter.

Okay, Bird, I said to myself. Now you got two choices. You can go on back to the Have-to-Have-It Shop like you planned, or you can go inside this tattoo parlor and make Harlem Tate be your friend.

I opened the door and went inside.

"Hey," I said. "What y'all doing?"

"Hey there," Ray said.

"Don't worry, I don't want a tattoo," I said, grinning.

Ray chuckled. Harlem had a look on his face that said, "You must be some kind of crazy girl, so get yourself on out of here."

But I didn't give him a chance to say it.

"What you doing?" I said.

Harlem's eyes flicked up at me from under his hair. "Making a sign," he said.

"What kind of sign?"

"For Ray."

Ray made a whooshing noise as he blew smoke up towards the water-stained ceiling. I sure wanted to stare at those colorful tattoos running up and down his arms, but I didn't.

I walked over to the counter and tilted my head to look at the sign in front of Harlem.

My design or yours, it said. *Possibilities endless. No design too complicated.* Under that was a list of some of the endless possibilities. Unicorn. Centaur. Submarine. Eagle. Orchid. Rattler. Lizard. Chalice.

I couldn't help but admire Harlem's writing. He didn't even need a ruler to keep the words and letters straight. And then it hit me. Wham! Harlem was writing those words all by hisself. And, believe me, those were some hard words. All this time, I'd been thinking Harlem wasn't too smart and now here he was, writing words like that! I mean, "centaur"? And "chalice"? "Orchid"? "Possibilities"? Shoot, I couldn't even spell "eagle."

Right here before my very eyes was my backup plan.

"Be my partner in the spelling bee," I said.

Harlem squinted at me for a minute and then shook his head and said, "Naw."

"How come?" I said.

Harlem started doodling in one corner of the poster.

"You already got a partner?" I said.

"No."

"Then be my partner."

Harlem shook his head. "No way."

"Why not? Did you see the prizes?"

"No."

"Didn't you read that paper we got?"

"No."

I reached into my sweatshirt pocket and pulled out the spelling bee paper. I had folded and unfolded it so many times it was beginning to tear. I put it on the counter in front of Harlem and smoothed the creases out.

"Read that," I said, jabbing a finger at the list of prizes. "And each person gets to pick three prizes," I added. "That's three for you and three for me."

Harlem didn't even look at the spelling bee paper. He just shook his head and went back to working on Ray's tattoo sign, drawing little red stars beside each word.

I pushed the paper closer to him. "Why not?" I said.

He kept his eyes on his little red stars and wouldn't even look at that list of prizes. " 'Cause I don't want to," he said.

"But *why?*" I heard my voice getting high and whiny. "You already got a partner?" I asked again.

He shook his head.

"Look how good you spell," I said, pointing to the word "centaur." "I bet that so-called genius Amanda Bockman can't even spell *that.*"

Harlem's star-drawing hand stopped moving and he sat up. I watched his face and in my mind I was saying, "Please, please, please." And then I saw it. One tiny little flicker on his face that told me maybe I had a chance.

"Shoot, you could win that spelling bee, for sure." I gave him a little poke in the arm. "All you need is a partner." I held my arms out and grinned. "And here I am."

I kept that grin on my face and tried to look calm and relaxed. But my insides were churning around like crazy. "Come on, Harlem," my mind kept saying. "Say yes. Please say yes."

Harlem looked at me and then down at that sign and then back at me and then he said, "Okay."

"Okay?"

He nodded. "Okay." Then he wiped his palms on his T-shirt, picked up a black marker, and started drawing a border of barbed wire along the edges of the poster.

I pumped my fist in the air and let out a "Yes!" Then I held my palm up so me and my new partner could slap each other a high five, but I guess Harlem didn't want to. He glanced up, but then went back to his drawing.

I carefully folded the spelling bee paper and put it back in my pocket.

"We can start tomorrow," I said. "Where do you want to meet?"

Harlem looked up at me through clumps of greasy hair. "Meet for what?" he said.

"To study."

"I don't need to study."

"Well, I sure do."

"Then study."

"But you're my partner. You have to help me."

Right away I heard my bossy tone and scrambled to change it. "I mean, I need you to help me. I'm not too good at spelling." I saw doubt dancing all over Harlem's face, so I quickly added, "I mean, I'm good, but not as good as you. If you help me, I'll be really good and then we can win those prizes. Which one you like? The bike?"

Harlem shrugged. "Yeah, I guess."

"So, you'll help me?" I lifted my eyebrows and set a smile on my face.

"Okay."

"You want me to come here on Monday?"

Harlem looked at Ray. Ray looked at the calendar on the wall behind him.

"I got a customer at four," he said.

"We'll be done by then," I said. I turned to Harlem. "Right here after school, okay?"

Harlem nodded and I charged out the door and skipped off down the sidewalk. I couldn't hardly believe I had me a friend and a ticket to Disney World, all wrapped up in one. I didn't care about the Have-to-Have-It Shop anymore. All I wanted was to get myself to Miss Delphine's and tell her that I had found a backup plan.

7

"Well then, I think we need to celebrate," Miss Delphine said. "Bird and Harlem, spelling bee partners." She took a carton of ice cream out of the freezer. Then she stood on tiptoe and peered into the cupboard, pushing aside soup cans and boxes of macaroni and cheese.

"Aha!" she said. "Here we go."

Cherries. Nuts. Chocolate syrup. She arranged them on the table in front of me.

We ate two bowls each.

"I figure if me and Harlem study every day after school, we'll be ready," I said. "That gives us three weeks and two days."

Miss Delphine tossed her spoon into her empty bowl with a clang and patted her stomach. Her hair was pinned up on top of her head with rhinestone clips. Curly wisps of hair framed her face.

"I'm proud of you, Bird," she said.

I popped one last cherry into my mouth. A little tornado of excitement was whirling around in my stomach. I'd been trying hard to keep my thoughts on the ground instead of soaring up into space and spinning out of control. If all you get out of this spelling bee is a friend, I told myself about a hundred times, then thank your lucky stars and be done with it.

But my greedy mind wouldn't stop at that. Before I knew it, I was going over that list of prizes in my head. Should I choose the karate lessons? I just couldn't decide. Then while I was pondering that, my thoughts would go skipping on down the road to Disney World. I pictured me and Harlem eating corn dogs and standing in line for Space Mountain. Harlem would want to go on all the same rides as me. He wouldn't complain one little bit if we went in the haunted house four times. And he wouldn't think I was a baby if I got Snow White's autograph. It would be perfect. Me and my friend, there at the Happiest Place on Earth.

At school on Monday, I couldn't keep myself from smiling nearly all day. Even when Hannah Bates told me I smelled like cat food, I kept on smiling like I didn't care. And you know what? Maybe I didn't care.

I tried to catch Harlem's attention at recess, but he was too busy shuffling his feet around in the dirt while the other boys played basketball. Once the ball landed near him and he picked it up. Everybody was waving their arms and hollering for him to throw them the ball. He threw it towards Jason Marks but missed by a mile, sending the ball bouncing off into the bushes. Everybody yelled names at him. Retard. Freak. Names like that.

When the afternoon bell rang, I raced down the hall.

"Harlem!" I yelled over the clang of lockers.

He looked in my direction but didn't stop.

When I caught up with him, I held up Miss Delphine's dictionary. "Look what I got."

"What's that for?"

"To study," I said. "Miss Delphine gave it to me."

We let the swarm of kids push us through the front door of the school, then moved on down the sidewalk away from them.

"You remember her," I said. "The one who brought the apple pie with me? She lives next door to me."

Harlem looped his thumbs through the straps of his backpack and glared down at the sidewalk. His long legs and giant feet took such big steps I had to jog to keep up with him. It was clear he wasn't going to talk much, so I shut up and just listened to the squeak squeak of his sneakers.

When we got to Elite Tattoos, Harlem threw his backpack in the corner. The smell of popcorn drifted out of the back room.

"That you, Sue Ann?" Ray called.

"It's me," Harlem said.

Ray pushed the curtain aside. A cigarette dangled

from the corner of his mouth. He squinted through the smoke. "Hey, buddy," he said. That seemed nice to me, Ray calling Harlem "buddy" like that. I bet Harlem liked it, too.

"Mr. Moody wants to see you," Ray said, making his cigarette bob up and down.

Harlem started up the stairs and I was right behind him. I was dying to see old Mr. Moody's place. But Harlem stopped so suddenly I ran into the back of him.

"Wait here," he said.

I shrugged like I didn't care and watched Harlem disappear up the dark stairway.

I climbed onto one of the stools at the counter.

"Who's Sue Ann?" I said.

Ray dropped his cigarette stub into a soda can. It sizzled when it hit the bottom.

"Friend of mine," he said.

"Has she got tattoos?"

Ray grinned. "A couple."

I watched him toss magazines into a cardboard box on the floor. Finally I had a chance to study his tattoos. A scaly green snake with glaring red eyes crawled down from his shoulder, winding around and around his arm. There was a black spiderweb on one elbow and letters on each of his fingers that spelled out "L-O-V-E" on one hand and "H-A-T-E" on the other. But the best tattoo was peeking out of the top of his shirt—an eyeball with wings.

We both looked up at the sound of footsteps on the floor overhead. A door closed and Harlem came downstairs. He unwrapped a grease-spotted napkin and laid it on the counter. Potato chips.

"Thanks," I said, reaching for a handful.

"So, how are we gonna study?" Harlem said.

I wiped a greasy palm on my jeans and took out the dictionary.

"Miss Delphine says we should start with 'A' and work our way to 'Z.' " I opened the dictionary and flipped to the start of the "A's." "I'll call out some words to you and then you call out some words to me."

And so it went. "Abacus. Accent. Admirable. Affectionate." Harlem getting them right and me getting them wrong.

But Harlem, he didn't get mad. He'd just shake his head and spell the word for me real slow.

"Now you spell it," he'd say.

And I'd spell it right and he'd say that was good and we'd move on to the next word. Harlem made a list of the ones I missed in a notebook and then every once in a while he'd call out one from the list. If I missed it again, he still didn't get mad. Just spelled it slow and waited for me to get it right.

Ray sat on a metal folding chair by the window, smoking and nodding and chuckling and looking out at the sidewalk every now and then. Waiting for Sue Ann, I figured.

We kept on. Word by word. "Assess. Atrocious. Attire. Authentic." By four o'clock my head was spinning and I was sure relieved when Ray said it was time for us to quit.

Harlem handed me the notebook. "Study these for tomorrow," he said.

I opened my mouth to ask him if he was crazy, but then for once in my life I had the good sense to hush up. I put the notebook in my backpack with the dictionary.

"See you tomorrow," I said.

That night, while Colleen talked on the phone to some boy who didn't even go to school (a secret I planned on using to my advantage someday), I propped my pillow up in bed and opened Harlem's notebook across my knees. I looked at the first word, then slapped my hand over it and looked up at the ceiling while I whispered the letters one by one. I lifted my hand just a crack and peeked at the word. I got it right. I felt a smile spread across my face.

I went down the list, from "abridged" to "assumption." I put a red mark by the ones I got wrong and I whispered those again.

Then I tucked the notebook under my pillow and closed my eyes. Harlem Tate might look mean on the outside, with that frown and those glaring eyes. But on the inside, he was someone being nice to me and helping me spell. Nothing mean about that, now, is there?

I ran over to Miss Delphine's, my backpack bumping so hard against me it like to knocked me over. When I got there, she was pushing Pop's wheelchair out onto the porch.

"It might be too cool out here for him," she said. She pulled his food-stained bathrobe closed and tucked a blanket over his lap. Pop's head bounced on his neck like a rag doll's. A string of drool dripped out of his mouth and landed on his hand. Miss Delphine whipped a tissue out of her pocket and wiped it off. Takes a good heart to do that, I thought.

"Are you too cool out here, Dad?" she said.

Pop shook his head and said, "No," with a gravelly kind of voice.

Miss Delphine patted his arm, and his crooked mouth turned up just a tad like he was smiling.

I tried to picture my own daddy in that wheelchair,

and then I worried that my heart wasn't nearly so good as Miss Delphine's.

"I'm going to Harlem's after school, so I won't be here today," I said. "I just thought I'd come by and say hey."

"Well, I'm glad you did," Miss Delphine said, combing Pop's hair real slow and gentle. "How's the spelling going?"

"We're doing 'B' today," I said.

I sat on the porch steps and watched her comb with one hand and smooth with the other. Comb and smooth. Comb and smooth.

"I just think this is so exciting, you and Harlem being together in that spelling bee and all," Miss Delphine said.

She didn't have her makeup on yet and she looked different. Younger. Like a kid, almost.

"Mitsy Rayburn and Jenna Little made two hundred flash cards," I said, trying not to look at Pop when he made mumbly noises.

Miss Delphine tucked the comb into the pocket of Pop's bathrobe and sat on the step beside me.

"Well, so what?" she said. "That don't mean diddly-squat."

"I guess."

She put her arm around me and squeezed. "Come on, now, my little Birdie," she said. "You got to have faith."

"Okay."

"I bet your mom and dad are proud as can be," she said.

I nodded. "Daddy's gonna change his truck-driving schedule so he can come to the spelling bee."

Miss Delphine smiled in that twinkly-eyed way of hers. She brushed my hair out of my eyes. "Let me give you a perm."

"No way."

"A body wave, then."

"Uh-uh."

"How about just a trim?"

"I tell you who could use a haircut," I said. "Harlem."

"Really?"

I nodded. "He looks like a hippie or something. I swear."

Miss Delphine laughed. "Then you bring him over here. I'll fix him up."

"I bet he won't come."

"Why not?"

"Well, what am I gonna say? 'Hey, Harlem, how come you want to look like a hippie? Why don't you let Miss Delphine cut your hair?'"

"Oh, I'm sure you'll think of something." Miss Delphine slapped my knee and stood up. "Now you better get yourself to school, Miss Bird."

That afternoon at Elite Tattoos, I sat across from Harlem at the card table by the window. Ray was at the counter, flipping through a magazine with race cars on the cover. It seemed like the tattoo business was kind of slow.

" 'Biennial,' " Harlem said.

I closed my eyes and used my finger to write invisible letters in the air. " 'B-I-E-N-E-A-L,' " I said, then opened my eyes just enough to peek at Harlem. His face told me I got it wrong.

Harlem wrote the word in his notebook and then spelled it for me, slow and patient, just like the others.

I slumped against the back of my chair. "We might as well give up," I said. "I can't do this."

"Okay." Harlem slapped his notebook shut and stood up.

"Good, then let's play checkers," Ray said.

I jumped up. "Wait a minute. You mean you're gonna quit? Just like that?"

"You're the one who quit," Harlem said.

"I did not!"

"Yes, you did."

"You did," Ray said, lining the checkers up on the checkerboard.

"Well, I didn't mean it," I said. "Jeez, y'all have to take everything I say so serious?"

Just then the bell over the door tinkled and Mr. Moody came in carrying a bulging garbage bag that clattered and clanged with every step. There must have been about a million cans in there. I wrinkled my nose. The smell of garbage and stale beer hovered in the air around that bag.

"Bring this upstairs," Mr. Moody said, thrusting the bag at Harlem.

Ray and I watched Harlem carry the clattering bag up the stairs behind Mr. Moody.

"I hate him," I said.

Ray lifted his eyebrows. "Who?"

"Mr. Moody."

"Why?"

"He's so mean," I said. "And he chews tobacco. That's gross."

Ray swept the checkers off the board and into a shoebox. "Aw, he just wants to be left alone."

I picked a checker up off the floor and tossed it into the shoebox. "All he ever does is hunt for cans," I said.

Ray lit a cigarette and blew a stream of smoke up to the ceiling. "He likes to fish," he said, snapping his lighter shut with a click.

"Where's he fish? I never saw him fishing anywhere."

"I took him out to my place at the lake once." Ray scratched his spiderweb elbow. "Maybe I'll take him and Harlem both out there sometime."

"I like to fish," I said.

Ray smiled, making his eyes crinkle up at the corners. "Then you come, too."

"How come Harlem lives with him, anyway?" I said.

"I'm not exactly sure."

"Didn't you even ask?"

"Mr. Moody pays his rent and stays out of my business, so I stay out of his," Ray said.

"Harlem's daddy's in prison and his mama choked on a chicken bone at the Holiday Inn," I said.

Ray laughed so hard he started coughing. "Is that right?" he said, wiping tears from his eyes.

I felt myself blush. "That's what I heard."

"I reckon that's as good a story as any."

"Then what's the real story?"

"Beats me," he said. "But I guaran-dern-tee you it's not as good as that one."

I've always been one to ask what I want to know, so it was against my nature that I hadn't just up and asked Harlem why he had come to Freedom and what he was doing living with Mr. Moody. I guess there was just something about him that told me to go slow.

But when Harlem came back downstairs, I knew I couldn't wait another minute.

"How come you're living with Mr. Moody?" I said.

A cloud moved over Harlem's face for one tiny second; then he said, "Family problems."

"What kind of problems?"

Ray cleared his throat and shuffled his feet around, but I ignored him.

Harlem shrugged and stooped his shoulders like he was trying to be smaller. "Just problems."

"Is Mr. Moody related to you?" I asked.

"Yeah."

"Do you like him?"

Harlem tossed his head to get the hair out of his face. "Yeah."

"Everybody calls him the Can Man," I said.

Harlem picked up the dictionary, thumbed through the pages until he got to the "B's," and said, " 'Boutique.' "

I took a deep breath, lifting my shoulders clean up to my ears and then letting them drop with a long, loud sigh. Then I pushed Harlem's notebook across the counter towards him and tossed him a pen.

"You might as well add that to the list," I said.

Harlem wrote "boutique" in his notebook and then he said, "You're doing good."

I felt my mouth drop plumb open. "I am?"

He pushed his hair out of his eyes and nodded.

"Really?" I said. I guess I wanted to hear him say it again.

"Really," he said.

He must have seen the doubt in my eyes, 'cause he said, " 'Boutique's' a hard word."

"Yeah," I said. " 'Boutique' *is* a hard word."

We weren't even finished with the "B's" yet and already I was beginning to think I really did have me a friend.

9

"Cable. Censor. Collapse. Compile." Me and Harlem were moving right along. When Ray didn't have a customer (which seemed like most of the time, if you ask me), we studied at the tattoo parlor, calling words out to each other from Miss Delphine's dictionary. Then I took Harlem's notebook home to study the words I'd missed. Harlem had only missed one word so far. "Cantaloupe." I'm sorry to say that when he missed that word, I couldn't help but bask in the thrill of it, jumping up and hollering, "Wrong! That's wrong! You got it wrong!"

Harlem had looked like he'd just sat on a bee—surprise and pain all wrapped up together—and I felt sort of bad that I hadn't been calm and patient like he was every one of the hundred times I missed a word. But I guess that was the difference between me and Harlem.

It seemed like a day didn't go by that I didn't marvel over how smart Harlem was. I couldn't understand why he wouldn't hardly say a word in school, why he just sits there and gets laughed at and acts like he don't know what's going on.

So one day I just up and asked him.

"How come you let everybody think you're dumb when you're not?"

His face got red and he said, "What do you mean?"

"I mean like today, when Mrs. Moore wrote those sentences on the board and she asked you to say which words were adverbs."

I sat in the back of the room near Harlem and I had seen all those faces smirking back at him. I had watched him slump down in his desk and shrug his shoulders. And I had known that if anybody in that room knew an adverb from a noun, it was Harlem Tate.

Now I watched his face and tried to read his thoughts, but I couldn't.

"I don't know," he said.

Harlem sure was a puzzle.

The day we started on the "F's," Ray got a love letter. I knew it was a love letter 'cause it reeked of perfume.

"Peee-yew," I said, holding my nose for effect. "I can smell that love letter from here." I fanned my other hand in front of my face.

Ray grinned.

"Is that from Sue Ann?" I said.

"Nope. Wanda Billingsley."

"You ever been married?"

"Twice." Ray tucked the letter into his shirt pocket and popped open a soda. "The first time 'cause I was stupid and the second time 'cause I was dumb."

"Ray was married to Miss South Carolina," Harlem said.

"Runner-up to Miss South Carolina," Ray said. "But Miss Nag-Me-to-Death-and-Spend-All-My-Money-in-One-Day would have been more like it."

Me and Harlem laughed.

"You ought to meet Miss Delphine," I said.

I wasn't sure what Miss Delphine would think about a man with a flying eyeball tattoo. But Ray was nice and Miss Delphine had a way of looking through the outside of a person and getting right on in to find the good part—the inside.

I gazed out the window and thought wouldn't it be nice if Miss Delphine and Ray met each other and then they liked each other so much that they got married. Ray would move into Miss Delphine's place and me and Harlem would go over there for dinner every night. And since my daddy is a truck driver and travels so much and Colleen is so hateful, Mama would say it was okay if I go live with Miss Delphine and Ray, so I do. And then Harlem gets fed up with that awful Mr. Moody, so he moves in over there, too. And then Miss Delphine and Ray adopt me and Harlem as their own and we all go to work in the tattoo parlor.

" 'Facilitate.' " Harlem interrupted my daydream.

"How come you want to look like a hippie?" I blurted out. "Why don't you let Miss Delphine cut your hair?"

Now, how come I had to go and say that out of the blue like that? Sometimes my mouth just decides to talk, and before I know it, I've gone and said something I wasn't even planning on saying.

Harlem's face got red and he looked down at his giant feet.

Now when I needed my mouth to say something, it wouldn't. Just clammed up and left me sitting there feeling bad.

"That's a good idea, Harlem," Ray piped in. "Maybe she can trim mine up some while she's at it."

I perked up. "Yeah, she could trim yours up some, too," I said. "But y'all have to go to her house. She can't leave her daddy unless her sister, Alma, comes over, and she lives clear over in Fort Valley."

Ray punched Harlem on the arm. "How 'bout that?" he said. "We'll get us a free haircut. Maybe I'll give her a free tattoo."

Me and Ray laughed, but Harlem, he just said, " 'Fluent,' " and turned to a fresh page in his notebook. I figured he was mad about being called a hippie, but I knew I could work the mad out of him pretty easy.

I knew Mama was going to have a hissy fit if I was late for dinner again like I always am, so I was trying to keep my mind on hurrying down the sidewalk. But spelling words kept kicking around inside my brain, slowing my feet down. "Facsimile. Forsythia. Fungus." How was I ever going to make it all the way to "Z"?

That's what was on my mind as I headed home and that's why I nearly jumped out of my shoes when Mr. Moody stepped out of the bushes right in front of me and I ran slap into him. Cans went every which way, rolling and clanging and spilling puddles of soda on the sidewalk.

I waited to be yelled at, but Mr. Moody didn't say one word. He just started picking cans up off the ground and tossing them back into his bag.

"I'm Bird," I said. "Remember me?"

He nodded. His shirt was unbuttoned, showing his gray-haired chest and his sunken-in stomach with his ribs sticking out. He sure was skinny. And guess what he had hanging from a string around his neck? A radio. I couldn't get over that. A beat-up–looking radio all held together with silver tape.

"Harlem's a good speller," I said, helping him pick up the cans.

Mr. Moody flung his garbage bag over his shoulder like Santa Claus with his sack of toys. I thought he was just going to walk away, but instead he said, "I never was much one for spelling." His wild-haired eyebrows danced up and down like they were alive.

"Me neither," I said.

Mr. Moody turned to go.

"I know where there's a bunch of cans," I said.

He turned back and looked at me. His whiskery face was tanned and leathery-looking.

"In that ditch that runs beside Faris Road," I said. "There's a bunch of 'em in there."

Mr. Moody's mouth twitched like it was just dying to smile, but didn't. He nodded his head at me, then turned and headed off down the sidewalk, his cans going clang, clang, clang in that bag.

"This is Ray and this is Harlem," I said with a good feeling in my stomach 'cause here I was with my three friends and it seemed like just yesterday I only had one. (That one being Miss Delphine, of course.)

Miss Delphine thrust a hand out towards Harlem. "Nice to meet you, Harlem," she said.

Harlem ducked his head in that way of his—like he wished he was short instead of taller than Miss Delphine. "Nice to meet you," he said. I knew he needed some time to warm up.

Then Miss Delphine turned to Ray and did the same thing, shaking hands and smiling and all, and ole Ray, he looked like he'd just floated through the pearly gates of heaven. Miss Delphine was wearing that fluffy white sweater that I love and the blue jeans with shiny silver studs down the sides. If that red-eyed snake crawling down Ray's arm bothered her, she didn't let on. (But I was kind of relieved to see that Ray had buttoned his shirt all the way up so that flying eyeball wasn't showing.)

"Who's first?" she said, waving her arm toward the kitchen chair she had put on a sheet in the middle of the living room.

Ray nodded at Harlem and Harlem looked kind of pitiful, but he went on over and sat down.

It was just like Miss Delphine to make that afternoon sail on by as easy as anything. She talked on and on about one thing or another and before long even Harlem was rattling on about how his favorite sandwich is pineapple on toast and how he used to go crabbing down in Savannah 'cause he has cousins down there.

Ray was nearly falling all over hisself handing Miss Delphine the scissors and saying "Yes, ma'am" and "No, ma'am" till she flapped her hand at him and said, "Stop that. You're making me feel old." (And then he's saying he's sorry about forty times too many.)

Finally, Miss Delphine says, "Ta-da!"—holding her arms out wide and grinning at Ray and Harlem.

And there they stood. The two of 'em. Brand-new haircuts. And Miss Delphine had done a fine job.

So Ray and Harlem are poking each other and mumbling thank yous and the next thing you know we're all playing cards and eating pretzels. Miss Delphine put on feathery pink slippers that showed her red-painted toenails and laughed a lot in that loud way of hers that makes everybody else laugh, too.

I called home to see if I could stay for dinner and Mama said no but I pretended like she didn't and stayed anyway. I knew she'd probably send Colleen over to get me and I'd be in trouble, but it felt so good being there at Miss Delphine's with Ray and Harlem that it was worth getting hollered at.

Miss Delphine heated up leftover spaghetti and some of Alma's homemade succotash. Ray and Harlem carried on about how tasty it was and how it sure hit the spot and things like that.

Once or twice Miss Delphine left the room to check on Pop, and Ray would whisper to Harlem how nice his haircut looked.

After dinner we played a spelling game that Miss Delphine made up and I couldn't believe how good I did, even though me and Harlem were only up to "H."

I know that night will stay with me till kingdom come—over there in Miss Delphine's house, playing games and eating pretzels with my three friends.

10

By the time we got to "L," Harlem knew that my daddy had been married once before, that I found Randy Buckner's math homework in the cafeteria last week (and threw it in the garbage 'cause he calls me names), and that I got eight stitches in my arm when I fell off the back porch with a steak knife last Fourth of July. He knew my favorite color, how many sit-ups I did in gym last year, and why Colleen's hair fell out when she was five.

But I still didn't know much of anything about Harlem. If there was a contest for changing the subject, Harlem would get the trophy, that's for sure.

But that didn't stop me from trying. About the most I could get out of him was that his uncle shot a cat one time and his cousin got kicked out of school for starting fires. No mention of his mama and the chicken bone yet.

" 'Likable,' " Harlem said.

"I know, I know," I said. "No 'e.' You've said that one a hundred times already."

"What about 'likely'?"

" 'L-I-K-E-L-Y.' Let's go spy on Ray." I looked at the curtain over the door leading to the back room. A big, fat man was back there getting a tattoo. Ray had let me and Harlem stay this time, and I was sure dying of curiosity about what it looks like to get a tattoo.

"Ray wouldn't like it," Harlem said.

"So?"

"So I don't want to."

"I'm sick of spelling," I said.

Harlem closed his notebook and laid his pencil down. "Then what do you want to do?" he said. "Besides spy on Ray."

I slammed the dictionary shut. "Let's go to the Have-to-Have-It Shop."

So me and Harlem headed on over there.

Mrs. Eula Thatcher was sitting in a dirty old chair eating biscuits and gravy that looked like dog slop (smelled like it, too).

"Who's that?" she said, jabbing her fork at Harlem and spattering drops of gravy onto her giant stomach.

"Harlem Tate," I said.

"Where's he from?"

"He lives with Mr. Moody."

She let out a big "Pffft" that sent spit and gravy flying every which way. "What's he living with that sorry sack of misery for?"

I felt bad that she said that, but Harlem just said, "You got any binoculars?" like he hadn't even heard her.

"Nope." Mrs. Thatcher pushed herself up out of her chair with a grunt and tossed her gravy-soaked paper plate into the trash. "Got a microscope," she said, taking a big, wheezy breath.

"You got any new stuff?" I said.

She flapped a hand toward the corner of the store.

I motioned for Harlem to come with me to rummage through the piles. We set to work, pushing stuff aside and picking things up. A waffle iron. Rusty cookie tins. A Monopoly game. A hair dryer.

"Hey, look," I said, stepping over a folding aluminum lawn chair. "Skates!"

I held up a pair of dirty white roller skates. They had black scuff marks on the sides, the laces were frayed and broken, and one of the fluffy pink pom-poms was missing. (They didn't smell too good, neither.) But that didn't stop me from slipping my foot into one and letting out a whoop when I saw it fit perfectly.

"I'm getting these," I whispered to Harlem.

I whispered 'cause I know Mrs. Thatcher's game. If you let on like you want something real bad, she won't budge one little cent off the price. But if you play like you don't give a hoot, then you might can get yourself a bargain.

So I worked on Mrs. Thatcher for those skates and, sure enough, I managed to get them for exactly what I had in my pocket—$3.50.

Now I had something to look forward to after spelling practice every day. I'd put on those skates and me and Harlem would head outside. Most times I got off to a jerky start, but then I'd settle down and glide along, my teeth chattering and my knees shaking on the bumpy sidewalk. Harlem liked to run beside me in his slow-motion, long-legged way, his giant sneakers hardly making a sound.

Sometimes I'd have to holler "Get out of the way" at somebody 'cause I wasn't too good at stopping. And Harlem, sometimes he'd run smack into somebody. We got our share of dirty looks, but we didn't care. Then just about the time my head got clear of all those spelling words, Harlem would say, "Let's go study some more."

Sometimes I could talk him into going on a little farther, but most times he'd just turn around and head on back, making me scramble to stop my rolling feet and turn around.

We were all the way up to "R" when Miss Delphine decided to have a spelling bee party. Well, not exactly a party. More like just supper at her house, but she made it feel like a party.

"Y'all bring your spelling words and I'll fix supper, okay?" she said. "We can decorate the living room and use a tablecloth and all. Oh, and candles. Lots of 'em.

We'll use those candles Alma gave me. And then we'll have a pretend spelling bee so y'all can practice."

I watched her take the knickknacks off the knickknack shelf, wipe each one with a rag, and lay it on the tattered living room rug. Then she ran the cloth around in circles on the top of the shelf and carefully returned each knickknack to its spot.

"Be sure you tell Ray to come, too," she said, lining up a little glass horse beside a jewel-covered music box.

"I will," I said.

Miss Delphine put a china hummingbird on one side of the shelf, then changed her mind and moved it to the other side.

"Only eleven days left," I said.

She put both her soft, warm hands on my cheeks. "Ain't this exciting?" she said.

"Yeah," I said. But inside I was saying, "How am I ever gonna remember that 'omitting' has two 'T's' or that 'orator' ends in 'O-R,' not 'E-R'? And how come spelling is so easy for Harlem? Seems like nothing comes easy for me except getting hollered at, laughed at, or lied to by all them hateful kids at school."

Miss Delphine put the last knickknack on the shelf: a china clown riding on a little tiny bicycle.

"Hey, I know what!" she said.

"What?"

"Let's dress alike for the spelling bee supper," she said. "You know, matching colors and all."

She grabbed my arm and pulled me down the hall towards her bedroom.

"Let's look through my closet," she said. I watched her face so smiling and happy as she jerked blouses and skirts and sweaters out of the closet and tossed them on the bed. She looked like a little girl—not a grownup lady. A little girl who might come to my birthday party or go skating with me.

I stood there and let her hold blouses up to me or drape sweaters over my shoulders and it was all I could do to keep from closing my eyes and folding my hands and saying, "Thank you, Lord, for Miss Delphine."

That night, laying in my bed with the headlights of passing cars gliding across my bedroom ceiling, I did just that. I closed my eyes and I folded my hands and I whispered into the darkness, "Thank you, Lord, for Miss Delphine."

And then I added, "Please help me get to Disney World. Amen."

11

"Don't be shy, now," Miss Delphine said. "There's plenty more." She pushed a bowl of black-eyed peas across the table towards Ray.

It looked to me like Ray Davis didn't have one ounce of shy in him when it came to eating. He hunched over his plate and wiped around the edge with a piece of bread, sopping up juice from the collard greens and stewed tomatoes. Then he folded a piece of ham like a taco and scooped in a big blob of pickle relish.

Harlem wrinkled his nose at me and I wrinkled mine back. But Miss Delphine, she smiled like she'd just been crowned Queen of the Universe.

"How about another deviled egg?" she said.

Ray looked up like he was surprised to see the three of us sitting there. "Huh?" he said, his cheeks bulging out with ham. "Oh, yeah. Don't mind if I do."

When he reached for a deviled egg, that scaly green

snake tattoo stretched out and then coiled back again like it was alive. Like any minute now it was going to come slithering right off his arm and into the collard greens.

Miss Delphine stood up and smoothed her short red skirt. Then she straightened the ruffles on her pink blouse and fluffed her curly hair. Her flowery perfume floated in the air around her.

We were wearing the same colors, but something told me we didn't look too much alike. The red-checked skirt Miss Delphine had given me to wear was pinned at my waist with a giant safety pin.

"Don't worry," she had said. "Nobody's gonna see that pin." Then she had pulled her pink sweater with the sparkly gold threads over my head and smoothed my hair.

"There," she'd said, standing back and examining her work. I still wasn't too sure about my look, but Miss Delphine put her arm around me and led me to the mirror. There we stood, side by side, her looking like a valentine beauty queen and me with my legs bowed out like the letter "O" and my toothpick arms dangling at my sides and my ears sticking out through my stringy hair. Miss Delphine had jiggled my shoulder and said, "Aren't we a sight for sore eyes?"

Ray and Harlem had showed up early, standing under the porch light with their new haircuts all combed down slick. They had brought a box of Krispy Kreme doughnuts, and Miss Delphine had squealed, "Lookit this, Bird. Doughnuts!" like she was thrilled to death even though she had made an apple pie, so we sure didn't need those doughnuts.

Me and Miss Delphine had decorated the living room with crepe paper streamers and flowers made out of pink tissues. We had cut alphabet letters out of construction paper and taped them on the walls and curtains. There was a checkered tablecloth on the table, with a vase of pink and red carnations in the middle. We lit candles and turned on the tiny white Christmas lights we'd strung over the windows, and that room I'd been in a thousand times looked like a brand-new fairyland.

Ray and Harlem had sat there with their eyes bugged out while me and Miss Delphine carried in bowl after bowl of steaming food. Miss Delphine brought Pop in and pushed his wheelchair up to the table. She tucked his napkin under his chin and smoothed his hair down with her hand. Then she said grace.

"Thank you, Lord, for this food we are about to receive, and please help Bird and Harlem get through the 'T' words. Amen."

We all laughed and then the eating started and I didn't think it would ever stop. Leastways, not for Ray. Even when Miss Delphine said, "I think Pop's probably ready for bed," Ray was still mopping pie crumbs off his plate with the back of his spoon.

Miss Delphine pulled Pop's wheelchair away from the

table and wiped his face. As they headed for the bedroom, Pop lifted a shaky hand and said, "Bye." He looked happy, like he was pleased as anything to be there at the spelling bee party.

When Miss Delphine finished helping Pop to bed, she grinned at us and said, "Now let's have a spelling bee."

"Don't go past 'S,' okay?" I said.

"I know, I know." Miss Delphine opened the dictionary. "Who's first? Ray, you keep score, okay?"

And so it started. Me on one team and Harlem on the other. By the time we got to "F," I was losing big-time and Harlem was starting to bug me, all slouched down on the couch with his legs stuck out halfway across the room, rattling off those letters like he was bored silly. When he missed "granddaughter" (only put one "d" in there. Ha!), I covered my mouth with my hand to hide my smile and Miss Delphine shot me a look.

Finally Miss Delphine called out "souvenir" and the last drop of minding-my-manners went right on down the drain.

"This is stupid!" I hollered. "I can't do this. We might as well forget it."

Then I stomped out of that fairyland room in my shiny black shoes that hurt my feet, and I made sure the door slammed hard behind me. I went out into the darkness and squatted by the magnolia tree, burying my head in my arms and waiting for Miss Delphine to come after me.

But she didn't. Harlem did.

"Bird?" he called into the darkness.

"Go away."

"Where are you?"

"Right in front of you, you idiot."

In the glow of the streetlight I could see Harlem groping his way across the yard, like a blind man.

"Go away," I snapped again.

He jerked his head in my direction.

"You got 'likable' right," he said.

I pulled Miss Delphine's skirt over my knees. My breath came out like little puffs of smoke in the cold night air.

"I'm too dumb," I said. "I can't do this."

"You got 'palmetto' and 'salary' and lots of them others you missed yesterday." He kicked at the rotting magnolia leaves on the ground beside me. "I want to win that spelling bee," he said.

"Yeah, well, that's too bad."

The muffled sound of music drifted out of Miss Delphine's house. Twangy, hillbilly music.

Harlem sat on the ground beside me. He smelled like onions and greasy fried stuff. "Please don't quit, Bird," he said in a shaky voice.

I peered at him, trying to see his face in the dark.

"What's the matter?" I said.

"Nothing."

The silence between us felt big and solid, like a wall.

Then wasn't it just like me to blurt something out of the blue and surprise us both.

"Why'd you come to Freedom, anyways?" I said.

"I had to."

"How come?" I hoped he wasn't going to say "family problems" again. I was tired of going slow with Harlem. After all, we were friends, weren't we? It was high time I knew more about him.

"My mom got a new husband," he said, laying back in the cold, damp grass. "Again," he added.

I waited.

"He don't like me much and they fight about it," he said.

"Oh." What else could I say?

"When he moved in with us, he said he didn't want no kids. My brothers were old enough to leave but I didn't have nowhere to go. But Lloyd—that's her new husband, Lloyd—he just didn't want nothing to do with me. So they kept fighting and the next thing you know, here I am in Freedom."

"Why are you living with Mr. Moody?"

" 'Cause he's my dad."

Talk about a shock! "That old man?" I said. I guess that wasn't too nice, but he *is* old.

"Yeah," Harlem said. "I ain't never even seen him before. My mom says I have, but I don't remember it."

Well now, I sure needed a minute to let that news sink in. I'd known Mr. Moody was Harlem's kin, but I sure

★ 65

never figured he was his *daddy*. My mind went back to all those times I'd watched Mr. Moody shuffling down the sidewalk with that big bag of smelly cans. Who would have ever thought he had a son down in Valdosta? Not me, that's for sure.

"Do you like living with him?" I said.

"Yeah."

"What if your mama wants you to go back home?"

"I ain't going back there."

We listened to that twangy music coming from Miss Delphine's. Harlem tossed a leaf into the air.

"I need to win that spelling bee," he said. "I want to show my dad I can do something good."

I nodded like I understood just how he felt. Then I figured I ought to reveal some bad stuff of my own to make him feel better, so I said, "My sister Colleen is really mean and she goes out with a boy who doesn't even go to school."

We sat there in the dark and watched Miss Delphine and Ray through the living room window, dancing a jitterbug kind of dance in the candlelight.

And then you know what we did? We ran all the way over to Elite Tattoos and got my skates and we took off down the dark, empty sidewalks of Freedom. That red-checked skirt was falling down below my knees, but I kept going, faster and faster, my skates clunking over the sidewalk cracks in a steady rhythm. Harlem ran along beside me, hollering out words.

" 'Emperor'!" he hollered.

" 'E-M-P-E-R-O-R,' " I hollered back.

" 'Factual'!"

" 'F-A-C-T-U-A-L.' "

" 'Propel'!"

" 'P-R-O-P-E-L.' "

And on and on. Up and down the sidewalk we went, hollering and spelling and hollering and spelling until my feet were tingling and my legs were burning.

When we finally stopped, we leaned over with our hands on our knees, trying to catch our breath.

Then Harlem said, "I bet we can get all the way to 'W' tomorrow."

"Yeah," I said. "I bet we can."

12

Miss Delphine raised her eyebrows. "Well, what do you know?" she said. "I'd've never guessed that in a million years."

I shook my head. "Me neither." I watched her mashing up peas for Pop. "Mr. Moody is so *old*," I said.

Miss Delphine poured some milk over the mashed-up peas. She wiped her hands on her sweatshirt that said *Foxy Lady* on the front. "I suspect he's not as old as he looks," she said, putting the bowl of peas on a tray. "I suspect he's crammed a lot of living into a short time." She lined up a row of pills on a napkin beside the peas. "That'll put lines on your face, for sure," she added.

"Mama said he used to live in a tent," I said.

"Really?"

I nodded. "Over there in that field behind the high school. And she said one time when he was looking for cans, somebody threw a beer bottle at him from a car and hit him right in the face."

Miss Delphine's eyes filled up with tears. "That's terrible."

I nodded. "Mama said she thinks Ray must've give him some kind of deal on that room over the tattoo parlor," I said, "or else how could he pay for it, since all he's got is can money?"

Miss Delphine's face got soft and mushy-looking. She shook her head and chuckled to herself. "That Ray," she said. "He's just the sweetest thing." She picked up the tray. "Don't go away. I'll be right back."

When she left the room, I looked around the kitchen. Pop's wheelchair sat in one corner, a tattered quilt folded neatly on the seat. A laundry basket piled high with smelly sheets was on the floor by the back door. The counter was cluttered with pill bottles, cans of soup, and tissue boxes. It sure seemed like a lot of work taking care of Pop. But I'd never, not once, heard Miss Delphine complain.

"There," she said, coming back into the kitchen with the tray. "Now, where were we? Oh, yeah, Mr. Moody and Harlem. That surely is something."

"I think it'd be awful to have a mean old man like that for a dad," I said. "Don't you think he's mean?"

Miss Delphine wiped mushy peas off the tray with a napkin. "I don't know," she said. "Maybe he's just a loner."

"I guess that chicken bone story was a big, fat lie," I said.

Miss Delphine nodded. "I guess so."

The next day at school, Mrs. Moore told us we were going to have a practice spelling bee. "Uh-oh," was my first thought. What if I mess up bad? But I looked at Harlem and he seemed so calm and sure, slouched down in his seat with his fingers drumming quietly on his desk. So I closed my eyes and tried to picture some of the words I'd been missing. "Ferocious. Insufficient. Provincial." I had letters swirling around in my head like bees around honey.

Mrs. Moore told us to get with our partners, and then she divided us into two teams. I stood next to Harlem and wished like anything I could hold his hand. Then Mrs. Moore told us to hush up and listen to the rules so we'd know what the real spelling bee was going to be like the next day.

"Team One partners"—she motioned towards our side of the room—"will compete against Team Two partners." She motioned towards the other side of the room. "When it's your turn, you may discuss the spelling of the word with your partner. You will then write the word on the easel you see in front of you. The partners on the other team must then take turns deciding whether or not the word on the easel has been spelled correctly. Partners will receive a point for each correct answer." She looked from one side of the room to the other. "At the end of the first round, the five partners with the highest scores will go on to the second round. Any questions?"

Everybody started talking and poking, and that goody-goody so-called genius Amanda Bockman started jumping up and down, clapping her hands and beaming around at everybody like she was already picking out her prizes.

Mrs. Moore told us to quiet down so we could get started. And then I looked at Harlem and something bad was happening right before my very eyes. His face was white and his eyes were glassy and his lips were quivery.

"Pssst." I tried to get his attention.

He was still as a statue.

I poked him with my elbow.

"What's the matter?" I whispered.

"I can't do this," he said.

I leaned over closer to him. "What?"

"I can't do this."

Now, didn't that beat all? I didn't know whether to laugh, cry, or slap him silly.

"What're you talking about?" I said, trying to keep my voice low and calm.

He shook his head, stiff, like a robot. "I don't think I can do this, Bird."

"Listen to me, Harlem," I snapped. "You're the best speller here. You know you are. *I'm* the one who oughta be worrying, not you."

But I could tell my words weren't getting through to him 'cause he just stared out at that easel with his face getting whiter by the minute. Then he raised his hand and waved at Mrs. Moore and said, "I don't feel good."

Everybody looked at him (and some kids laughed). The next thing I knew, he was gone and I was left standing there wishing I really *was* a bird so I could fly right on out the window.

I shoved the door of the tattoo parlor open and stormed inside.

"Where's Harlem?" I said.

Ray came out of the back room. "What's the matter?"

"Is Harlem up there?" I jerked my head towards the stairs.

"I think so."

I started for the stairs and Ray said, "Whoa, now. I think you better count to ten first."

But I ignored him and stomped on up the stairs. Before I got to the top, Harlem came out of Mr. Moody's place and sat on the top step.

"What'd you do that for?" I hollered up at him.

He rested his elbows on his knees and put his chin in his hands. He wouldn't look at me.

"I didn't feel good," he said.

"That's a lie."

He still wouldn't look at me and I felt my face getting

hotter by the minute. "I had to stay there and spell by myself and I messed up after only two words."

He finally looked at me. "What word did you miss?"

I shoved him with both hands, making his feet fly up and his hands flail out and his mouth drop open in surprise.

"You said you wanted to win that spelling bee," I yelled. "Well, I do, too. Okay?"

He hung his head like a little kid. "I can't do it," he said.

"Why not?"

He shook his head. "I just can't."

I closed my eyes and took a breath. Then I sat on the step next to him. I made my voice come out as calm as I could. "Yes, you can," I said. "You know every one of those words. You can beat everybody."

"I mess up everything I do," he said.

I sighed. I wished Miss Delphine was there to help me know what to say.

"We can win this spelling bee," I said. "I know we can. And then we can get those prizes."

He shrugged.

"What prizes are you going to pick?" I said, trying to make my voice sound like someone who can win a spelling bee.

"I don't really care about them prizes."

When I heard that, my insides started to boil up and I

wanted to holler at him. But when I saw his face, I changed my mind. He looked like somebody had thrown a blanket of sad over him. I hadn't had a lot of practice being a friend, but I knew enough to know he didn't need to be hollered at.

"It seems like I can't do nothing right anymore," he said.

"Come on, Harlem," I said. "You can do this. You're a real good speller." I watched his face but I couldn't tell if anything was changing inside his head. "Besides," I added, "I need you. I can't do it without you."

He shook his head. "I don't think I can."

"Come on. I'll help you. We're partners, remember?" I nudged him on the shoulder. "And just think, when you win, you'll be like a hero or something. Everybody'll say how smart you are." I nudged him again. "Especially your daddy," I added.

I waited. I could hear Ray rustling the newspaper down in the tattoo parlor. The smell of bacon seeped from under Mr. Moody's door, making my stomach growl.

"Okay," Harlem said. "I'll try."

I let my breath out with a whoosh and slapped Harlem's knee. "Okay?" I said.

"Okay."

"That's good." I stood up. "I'm starving. I'm going home for supper. See you tomorrow."

I started down the stairs, but before I got to the bottom, Harlem called out, "Bird?"

I turned. "What?" I was hoping like anything he
wasn't going to change his mind.

"What word did you miss today?" he said.

" 'Compatible.' "

Then I headed on down the stairs and out the door,
with Harlem calling after me, " 'C-O-M-P-A-T-I-B-L-E.' "

13

The next day we all lined up while Mrs. Moore matched up partners. Then we marched down the hall and into the auditorium and right up onto the stage. I guess my legs were moving, 'cause there I was up there with everybody else, but I sure couldn't feel anything but those butterflies fluttering around inside my stomach.

My mama and daddy and Miss Delphine and Ray were out there somewhere, but I kept my eyes on the floor in front of me. We separated into two groups, one on each side of the stage, and sat in the folding metal chairs lined up there. I was wearing one of Miss Delphine's T-shirts that she had given me 'cause it shrank in the dryer. It was bright pink, with *Girl Power* in sparkly silver letters across the front. I loved wearing that T-shirt 'cause all day it made me think about Miss Delphine and feel good about myself. And I sure did need to feel good about myself that day.

I focused on a wad of gum hardened on the chair in front of me. "Don't throw up, Bird," I told myself a million times. My stomach was flopping around like a trout on a riverbank. And as if my flopping stomach wasn't enough to worry about, I had to worry about Harlem. He hadn't hardly said a single word since we'd got to school that morning. He had just slumped down in his chair and drooped his shoulders over like he was trying to disappear.

Mrs. Moore blew into the microphone and said, "Testing." A shrill screech came through the speakers and we all slapped our hands over our ears. Finally all the giggling and carrying-on stopped and the spelling bee started.

I concentrated on the words that Mrs. Moore called out, spelling them in my head, studying them on the easel, trying like anything to get them right.

When it was our turn, me and Harlem stood up. I couldn't hardly believe it when I saw who was on the other team against us. Mitsy Rayburn and Jenna Little, those girls who had made about a billion flash cards. Just my luck.

Mrs. Moore called out, " 'Appendix,' " and Mitsy and Jenna put their heads together and whispered. Then Jenna wrote "A-P-P-E-N-D-I-X" on their easel.

Mrs. Moore turned to me. "Bird, is the word 'appendix' spelled correctly?"

I pressed my lips together and looked hard at that

word. Then I looked up at the ceiling. "One 'P' or two?" I asked myself. I took a breath and said, "Yes, it's spelled correctly."

Mrs. Moore nodded and made a mark on her clipboard. "Correct," she said and I think people out in the auditorium were clapping, but I was too nervous to know for sure.

I grinned at Harlem, but he didn't even look at me. He stood there with his arms dangling down by his sides and glared over there at Mitsy and Jenna.

Then Mrs. Moore called out the next word, and me and Harlem got to whisper together about how to spell "visually." I just went along with whatever Harlem said and wrote it on the easel the way he told me to. Mitsy didn't even wait one second before saying, "That's correct."

Mrs. Moore nodded and made another mark on her clipboard. Then she called out, " 'Larynx.' " Jenna whispered in Mitsy's ear and Mitsy whispered in Jenna's ear. Then Jenna wrote "L-A-R-I-N-X" on their easel and my heart leaped with joy.

Me and Harlem had studied that word more times than I could count. " 'Y-N-X,' " Harlem had said in that patient way of his. " 'L-A-R-Y-N-X.' " He had circled it with a red pen in his notebook. Then, it seemed like nearly every day, he was calling that one out to make sure I got it right.

So I couldn't help but breathe easy and smile when I saw that word over there on their easel.

Mrs. Moore said, "Harlem, is the word 'larynx' spelled correctly?"

I waited for Harlem to say, "No, it is *not* correct," but instead, there was silence.

When I looked at him, my joyful heart sank with a thud. His chin was poked out and his eyes were squeezed up and he was leaning forward like he was going to fall right over the chair in front of him.

"Uh," he said, narrowing his eyes even more. "Um." He tried to take a step forward, running into the chair in front of him with a clang.

It seemed like forever that everything was quiet and then everybody was giggling and Mrs. Moore was saying, "Shhhh." Then she repeated, "Harlem? Is the word 'larynx' spelled correctly?"

And then Harlem said, "Yes, it's spelled correctly."

My mouth flew open and I jerked around to look at him. His cheeks were red and splotchy, and sweat was running down the side of his face.

"I'm sorry, Harlem," Mrs. Moore said, "but 'larynx' is not spelled correctly."

I watched Mitsy and Jenna hug each other.

Then Harlem walked across the stage and down the steps and up the aisle and right on out the auditorium door.

Just like that.

14

It took me a minute or two to figure out that the buzzing in my ears was people talking to each other. Folks were wagging their heads and turning around to look at the door in case Harlem changed his mind and came back. But he didn't.

Mrs. Moore said, "Well, now . . ." and looked at me like I was supposed to do something.

So I stood up and walked across the stage and down the steps and up the aisle and right on out the auditorium door.

Outside, I looked around, squinting in the bright sunlight. My mind didn't have a clue where Harlem could be, but my feet started walking anyway.

I'd only gotten as far as the bottom of the front steps when someone behind me called out, "Where you going?"

I turned around. Mr. Moody stood in the door of the

school. He looked so out of place there at school that it took me a minute to realize it was him. Mr. Moody had come to see Harlem in the spelling bee! How about that?

"I'm going to look for Harlem," I finally managed to say.

When I got to Elite Tattoos, I peered in the front window. It was dark inside. I jiggled the door handle. Locked. A sign on the door said CLOSED.

I stepped back and looked up at the second-floor window.

"Harlem!" I called up to the window.

No answer.

"Hey, Harlem, it's me, Bird."

Nothing.

I kicked the door, then jumped when a voice behind me said, "He might be upstairs."

Mr. Moody shuffled toward me. He had that radio tied around his neck again and, get this, he was wearing bedroom slippers.

"It's locked," I said.

Mr. Moody tugged on a dirty string tied to his belt and a key came out of his pocket. He unlocked the door and disappeared inside the tattoo parlor.

"You coming?" he called through the screen door.

By the time I got inside, he was halfway up the stairs. I waited at the bottom, peering up after him. He turned and called down, "You coming up or just standing there?"

"I'm coming," I called, hurrying up after him.

We stepped inside his room and I got the next shock of the day. That room was the best place I'd ever seen in all my born days. The walls were painted pure sky blue. Plants sat on shelves and trailed along tabletops. Tiny silvery fish darted around a fish tank by the window. It seemed like everywhere I looked was a cat, curled up on stacks of newspapers, stretched out on the lumpy couch, sleeping on the windowsill beside dirty coffee cups and cereal bowls.

In one corner of the room was a birdcage. Inside it, two little yellow birds pecked at a bell and chirped the prettiest bird chirps I ever heard. Plants and fish and cats and birds were enough to make me love this room, but there was something else that made me think I wanted to stay there forever. Pieces of glass in all shapes and sizes hung from the ceiling on glittering gold threads. They swayed in the breeze from the open window, and when the sunlight hit them, rainbows danced all around the room. Across the sticky linoleum floor. Over the cot piled with rumpled sheets. Even along the tops of my shoes as I stood there taking everything in.

"He's not here," Mr. Moody said. I jumped. I'd been so caught up in that room I'd nearly forgotten why I was there.

"How come Harlem to run off like that?" he said. He lifted a cat off of a rocking chair and sat down. I watched him set that cat back down on his lap and stroke it, and

I couldn't help but ask myself if this was that same mean old man with sugar die-bee-teez.

"I don't know," I said. "I don't understand it. He's the best speller I know. We practiced every day. He wanted to win."

Before I knew it, I was crying. I stamped my foot, making the birds flutter around their cage and scatter birdseed onto the floor.

"This was my one chance," I said. My throat was all squeezed up. "I should've known he wasn't really my friend. Why'd he do this to me, anyway?"

Mr. Moody stroked that cat and looked up at me from under his bushy eyebrows. "I reckon you'll have to ask him."

I knew I didn't have a right to be mad at Mr. Moody, but I was. I glared at him, stomped my foot one more time, then turned and headed back down the stairs as fast as I could.

15

I went around back to the alley that ran behind Elite Tattoos. Big green Dumpsters overflowing with plastic trash bags and cardboard boxes lined the alley. It smelled like rotten food and gasoline and something burnt, all mixed together. A mangy old dog ran by me with his tail between his legs.

"Harlem," I called out.

It was so quiet back there I could hear the flies buzzing around the garbage. Somebody had set a ripped-up teddy bear on top of a metal garbage can. I almost picked it up, but then I saw it had ketchup on it, so I didn't.

And then something caught my eye and I turned to look, and guess what? There was Harlem, sitting on an old couch cushion by the back door of Elite Tattoos.

"Hey," I said.

He glared up at me in that way of his, like he was mad. "Hey," he said.

Now what? I felt mad and confused and worried all at the same time and I didn't know which one to focus on first. I sat on the cushion beside Harlem and waited till my heartbeat settled down and I could get some calm back inside myself. Then I said, "Why'd you do that to me, Harlem?"

"I don't know," he said.

And that's when the mad came busting out of me and I punched him so hard he fell sideways. When he straightened back up, he rubbed his arm and blinked at me. Then he looked away.

"Why'd you do that to me?" I said again. "You knew that word. I know you did."

Harlem picked at the stuffing poking out of the couch cushion.

"Spell 'larynx,'" I said.

"'L-A-R-Y-N-X,'" he said in this tiny little voice.

"See! I *told* you. Why'd you say it was right when it was wrong? Even I knew it was wrong. I bet everybody knew it was wrong."

Harlem pulled at that stuffing, making a little mound of puffy cotton on the seat beside him. "It looked right to me."

"What do you mean it looked right? How could it look right?"

"It just did, okay?" Harlem snapped.

I sighed and shook my head.

"I can't do nothing right anymore," he said. "I didn't

miss that word on purpose, Bird. If that stupid easel had been closer, I could've got it right."

"What do you mean?"

"I mean that stupid teacher put that stupid easel too far away."

"You mean you couldn't *see* it?"

Harlem flicked his finger at that fluffy cotton mound, sending puffs of cotton drifting across the alley. "Not real good," he said.

"Well, why didn't you say so?"

He shrugged.

"Maybe you need glasses," I said.

"Naw." He shook his head.

"Harlem, if you couldn't even see that word good enough to know it was spelled wrong, you must need glasses. I could see it plain as day."

"You could?"

I nodded. "Yeah, plain as day. Didn't you ever notice your eyes before?"

"No. Well, maybe. A little."

I pointed. "Can you see that teddy bear over there?"

He squinted up the alley. Then he looked down at his feet and shook his head.

"You definitely need glasses," I said.

Harlem picked at his shoelace. "Maybe they'll get better," he said. "My eyes, I mean. I think I've been noticing them getting better."

"How long have they been bad?"

"I don't know."

"Why didn't you say something to somebody?" I said. "Your mama or somebody?"

Harlem rested his chin on his knees and gazed out across the alley. The back of his neck was white and freckled. Little tiny hairs were starting to grow back where Miss Delphine had used the hair clippers.

"I didn't want to cause trouble for my mom and make her mad at me," he said. "I didn't want her to fight with Lloyd."

"Why would she get mad about your eyes?"

"She just would have," he said. "When I started making bad grades and my teachers would call home, Lloyd would go crazy. He'd say I was dumb and all. And he'd yell at my mom and she'd cry and stuff 'cause of me."

Harlem tossed another cotton puff into the air. That mangy dog came trotting back up the alley towards us. It stopped to root through a trash bag, then sat down to enjoy a half-eaten sandwich.

"One time the school nurse called my mom and told her I should have my eyes checked," he said.

"What'd she say?"

"She got mad at me. She said why was I all the time causing trouble for her and Lloyd. She cussed at me and threw a can of pork and beans clear across the room."

My mouth dropped open in amazement and my mind

set to work picturing those pork and beans sailing through the air towards Harlem. I wondered if he had ducked, and if he did, what did that can of pork and beans hit? Maybe Harlem had caught the can and hurled it back and whapped her right upside the head and she fell down dead right there in the kitchen.

I confess to feeling a tad guilty when my insides got stirred up with excitement over the prospect of telling everybody at school the real story about Harlem's mama. "She didn't choke on a chicken bone," I'd tell that snooty Celia Pruitt. "She got hit with pork and beans."

I watched a bushy-tailed cat walk along the edge of a Dumpster, then run off when some lady opened a window and shook out a dusty rug. Somebody opened a door and tossed an empty cardboard box into the alley. I was hoping Harlem would tell me some more about that pork and beans story, but he didn't.

"Everybody thinks I'm stupid," he said.

"Not me."

"Do you really think I might need glasses?"

"Yeah, I think you might."

That mangy dog finished the sandwich and pawed at the trash bag, looking for some more good stuff to eat.

"Why don't you tell Mr. Moody?" I said.

Harlem shook his head. "No way. I want to stay here. I don't want him to send me back."

"Why would he do that?"

" 'Cause he doesn't have much money. He can't pay for stuff for me." Harlem shook his head again. "No way. I want to stay here. I don't want to mess up."

The dog had found something nasty-looking in that trash bag. A rotten smell drifted our way.

"I'm sorry I messed up the spelling bee for you," Harlem said. "I thought maybe I could do it."

"That's okay."

"I reckon you really wanted that bike."

I shook my head. "Actually, I wanted to go to Disney World."

"Really?"

"I guess that was crazy, huh?"

"I don't think so," he said.

"You don't?"

"No."

"You ever been to Disney World?"

"Naw."

"Ever want to?"

"Sure. I guess." He squinted across the alley at the dog. "I'm sorry I messed up. I didn't know you wanted to go to Disney World."

"That's okay." I thought about telling him about my other wish. My fame and glory wish. But I decided not to.

"Too bad about your eyes," I said.

"Yeah."

And there we sat. Side by side on a dirty old cushion, there behind Elite Tattoos. I guess we must have looked as pitiful as we felt, sitting there with that mangy dog and thinking about how the whole world was all filled up with wanting and not one little ounce of getting.

16

"Well, bless his heart," Miss Delphine said when I told her about Harlem and his bad eyes and those pork and beans and all. "That's just pitiful."

I nodded. "I know it."

Miss Delphine pushed a fluffy curl away from her face. "What are you going to do?"

"*Me?*"

"Yeah. You got to do something."

"Why me?"

Miss Delphine put her hands on her waist. " 'Cause he's your friend."

I guess I was so new at having somebody besides Miss Delphine for a friend that I hadn't realized I was supposed to do something. But what was I supposed to do?

"What am I supposed to do?" I said.

"I don't know," Miss Delphine said. "*Something*. You

can't just sit back and let that boy suffer like that. He's your friend. He needs help."

I propped my elbows on the kitchen table and rested my chin on my hands. Dried-up oatmeal from Pop's breakfast stuck to the table in splotches. I was glad it was Saturday, so I didn't have to watch Amanda Bockman flashing that shiny gold spelling bee medal all over school and bragging about all her prizes. (She picked encyclopedias. Can you believe that?)

"I think Harlem should tell Mr. Moody about his bad eyes," I said.

Miss Delphine jabbed a finger at me. "I think you're right."

"But then what if Mr. Moody sends him back to Valdosta?"

Miss Delphine lowered her head and looked up at me through her curly hair. "Do you think that's what Mr. Moody would do?"

I shrugged. "I don't know. But what if he did? Besides, Mr. Moody's poor. He can't buy glasses for Harlem, anyways."

"Lots of poor people have glasses, Bird."

"How do they get them?"

Miss Delphine stirred sugar into her coffee. "I'm not sure," she said. "But I know there are ways."

"What kind of ways?"

"I don't know. Like the Lions Club or something." She took a sip of her coffee, squinting through the steam that drifted up into her face. "I know there are ways for folks who need glasses to get them," she said.

"If you had a kid who needed glasses and you didn't have any money, what would you do?"

Miss Delphine tapped her fingernail against her coffee mug. "Well, I suppose I'd start with school," she said. "I'd talk to a teacher or a nurse or a principal or someone like that. Trust me, Bird, there's plenty of kids who need help getting glasses."

"There is?"

She nodded. "Probably."

That night I laid in bed thinking about Harlem. I'd wanted a friend for so long and now I finally had one and everything was all messed up. What if Harlem *did* have to go back to Valdosta? Then where would I be? Right here in Freedom, Georgia, with nobody at school to be my friend, just like before, that's where.

That thought made me feel pretty sorry for myself. I laid there trying to think about my pitiful situation, but I couldn't concentrate 'cause Miss Delphine's words kept jumping into my thoughts.

"Okay, Bird," I told myself. "You wanted Harlem to be your friend. Now he is, and he needs help."

Then I laid there and thought some more. I thought and thought and thought. And by the time I fell asleep that night, I knew what I had to do.

17

The next day after Sunday school, I went over to Elite Tattoos. It's closed on Sundays, but sometimes Ray sleeps in the back room if he doesn't feel like driving home to his trailer out at the lake. But that day, he wasn't there and the CLOSED sign hung on the door. I peered inside. Nobody. I stepped back and looked up at Mr. Moody's room. The window was open, even though it was starting to get cold out. I could hear those little yellow birds chirping. Church music drifted out the window. I wondered if it came from that little radio Mr. Moody wore around his neck.

I cupped my hands around my mouth and called up to the window. "Harlem?"

No answer.

I called again. Finally Harlem's face appeared in the window. When he saw me, he stuck his head out and called down, "I'll be there in a minute."

"I'll be around back," I said.

I sat on the old couch cushion and waited for Harlem. In a few minutes, I heard his giant sneakers slapping on the asphalt alley. I watched him walking towards me with his shoulders stooped over. His hair stuck up on one side and he kept pushing it down, but it just popped right back up again.

"Hey," I said.

"Hey."

"Amanda Bockman and Tanya Hooper won the spelling bee," I said and then wished I hadn't. Harlem's face got that sad-dog look and made me feel bad. "But who cares?" I added, setting a smile on my face.

He sat on the cushion next to me. He smelled good. Like soap or something.

"You've got to tell Mr. Moody about your bad eyes," I said.

He shook his head. "Uh-uh."

"You've got to, Harlem. He can help you get glasses and then everything will be okay."

Harlem snorted. "Yeah, right."

I could feel the mad starting to bubble around inside me, but I tried to settle it down. I made my voice sound real calm and patient. "He won't send you away," I said.

"How do you know?"

I scrambled around in my head to try to come up with an answer. "I think maybe he likes having you here."

Harlem snorted again.

"Shoot," I said. "As long as I can remember, he never did anything but look for cans. I've never seen him go anywhere till I saw him at the spelling bee."

Harlem jerked his head towards me. "He was at the spelling bee?"

I nodded. "He was. I saw him."

"Are you sure?"

"I talked to him. He helped me. He unlocked the door and helped me look for you."

"He did?" He narrowed his eyes at me, and I could see the doubt sneaking around inside his head.

"He invited me upstairs," I said. "I saw all those plants and cats. And those birds." I watched Harlem's face and saw the doubt starting to disappear. "And all that glass hanging around making rainbows and all," I added.

And then a miracle happened. We heard a familiar clanging noise and we looked up, and who do you think was walking up the alley towards us? That's right. Mr. Moody. Clang, clang, clang went that bag as he headed our way. Then he stopped to peer into a garbage can.

"Hey, Mr. Moody," I called.

He looked up. When he saw me and Harlem, he nodded in our direction, then shuffled over to another garbage can. He was wearing those ratty bedroom slippers again.

I nudged Harlem. "Go on," I said. "Tell him."

Harlem looked like he had thoughts all racing around inside his head. I nudged him again. "Go on. Do it."

And then I saw it. A little flicker in Harlem's eyes that told me he was right on the fence. Could go one way. Could go the other. So I did what I had to do. I jumped up and ran over to Mr. Moody and I grabbed his arm.

"Harlem wants to tell you something," I said.

Mr. Moody looked at me and for the first time I noticed how blue his eyes were. Pale blue and kind of watery, but nice. He squeezed his bushy eyebrows together and looked over at Harlem.

I wondered if he saw the same thing I did. I saw a sad-looking boy all slumped over on a dirty couch cushion with his long legs drawn up and his chin resting on his knees, looking like he'd never known a happy day in his whole life.

Mr. Moody shuffled over to him and put his bag of cans down. Then he sat on the cushion next to Harlem.

And that's how I left them, sitting there in that alley on the cushion. A sad boy and a tobacco-chewing old man. And I hoped like anything I hadn't messed up.

18

Miss Delphine and I waited on the front porch even though it was cold and damp outside. It had rained all day and had finally settled down into a gray mist.

"There he is!" Miss Delphine squealed, pointing up the sidewalk. "He's coming!"

We watched as Harlem jogged towards us through the puddles and soggy leaves. His sneakers squished as he climbed the porch steps. He stood straight and tall, not hunched over like usual. He grinned at us, blushing.

He was wearing his new glasses. Shiny wire glasses with thick lenses.

Miss Delphine clapped her hands together and carried on about how handsome he looked.

I nodded. "You look good," I said.

I wasn't just saying that to be nice. He really did look good. But it wasn't just his glasses that made him look good. He looked like a big gust of wind had come along and blown away that big black cloud that had been hovering there over his head. And I have to admit, I felt like my own black cloud had blown away, too. I'd worried and worried that day I left Harlem and Mr. Moody in the alley. What if Mr. Moody *did* get mad about Harlem needing glasses? What if he *did* send Harlem back to Valdosta? But he didn't. You know what he did? He went straight over to school the very next day and talked to the principal. Imagine that!

And now here was Harlem on Miss Delphine's front porch wearing his new glasses.

As I watched his face all smiling and nice-looking, I realized that all those times when he looked like he was glaring at the world out of meanness, well, he was just trying to see, is all.

"Let's go inside and celebrate," Miss Delphine said.

So the three of us, we went inside and Miss Delphine made hot chocolate with marshmallows. Harlem's glasses got steamed up when he drank his and we all laughed.

Then Miss Delphine called Ray and he came over with pizza. We sat on the living room floor and ate right out of the box. Every now and then, Harlem's hand would flutter up and touch his glasses.

Then we played Monopoly and Harlem told about a hundred knock-knock jokes. And I swear, if a feeling was a thing you could see, you would've seen nothing but happy all over that room that day.

Everybody laughed the first day Harlem wore his glasses to school. Big, sputtery laughs they didn't even try to hide. But Harlem didn't care and everybody knew it. He stood up straight and tall and he walked slow and sure and his face had a look of pure contentment. He strolled down the hall nodding and smiling at kids who had stuck gum on his back just the day before.

From the back of the class, he waved his arms at Mrs. Moore, wanting to answer each and every question she wrote on the blackboard. Kids turned in their seats in gape-mouthed wonder. Here was Harlem Tate, that stupid boy who never did anything right, turned into a genius overnight.

It wasn't even a week till kids were asking Harlem for answers on their homework or if he would be their science partner. But you know what? Harlem would say, "Naw, I got a partner." I'd look at him, wondering who his partner was, and then I'd realize he was talking about me.

Before long, it was clear that the door to the world of being-liked-and-treated-good was opening a tiny crack wider for Harlem every day. And then one day something happened that busted that door down altogether.

It was one of those days when me and Harlem didn't have much to do after school. We were tired of my skates and Ray had a tattoo customer. Miss Delphine had taken Pop to the doctor over in Macon. So we hung out on the school playground, not doing much of anything but kicking rocks and watching kids play basketball.

When the ball came rolling over the cracked and crumbling asphalt towards us, Harlem picked it up. He held it in one of his giant hands as easy as holding an orange. Then he bent his knees, and the next thing you know he was shooting way up off the ground and that basketball was hurtling through the air so fast it nearly whistled. And then—plunk—right onto the rim of the net, ricocheting up into the air, ten, twenty feet . . . and then straight back down, swish, right through it.

Everybody just stood there, looking at Harlem and then at the net and then back at Harlem again.

"I didn't know you could do that," I said.

"Why do you think they call me Harlem?"

"What do you mean?"

"Harlem Globetrotters," he said. "The basketball team?"

"Really?"

"I used to play basketball with my brothers all the time," he said. "Sometimes we didn't even go to school. Just played ball all day long. But then I couldn't play too good anymore, because of my bad eyes, I reckon, and my brothers would get mad." He pushed his glasses up higher on his nose. "But they still called me Harlem," he added.

It wasn't any time at all before Harlem was on the school basketball team. After that, those pea-flicking kids at lunch started making room for him at their table. But he'd always remember to scoot over and pat the bench beside him and say, "Sit here, Bird." I'd smile at all those kids and offer them some of my potato chips, but most times they wouldn't hardly even look at me. I think there was still a wall between us that even Harlem couldn't tear down.

The day before the first Freedom Middle School basketball game, I sat in Miss Delphine's beat-up lounge chair and watched her ironing Pop's pajamas.

"Alma's coming tomorrow at four," she said. "Why don't you come on over here about four-thirty and we'll wait for Ray?"

"Okay."

"What about Harlem? Does he need a ride?"

I shook my head. "He's going early to practice with the team."

Miss Delphine sprayed water on Pop's pajamas as she ironed, sending steam curling up towards the ceiling.

"I was thinking about something," I said.

"What's that?"

"I was thinking maybe we should see if Mr. Moody wants to go to the game with us."

Miss Delphine stopped ironing. "Well, of course we should," she said. "I can't believe I didn't think of that.

See how good you are, Miss Bird, always thinking of things like that?"

So I went over to Elite Tattoos and knocked on Mr. Moody's door. He looked kind of surprised to see me.

"Would you like to go to the basketball game with me and Ray and Miss Delphine?" I said.

His mouth twitched some and his eyebrows danced around a little and he nodded just a little bit and said, "I would."

So the next night, we all piled into Ray's car and headed over to Freedom Middle School. (I was glad to see that Mr. Moody wasn't wearing those bedroom slippers or that radio tied around his neck.) When we walked into the gym, I saw kids poking each other and laughing at us, but I pretended like I didn't. I just walked right on by them with Ray and Miss Delphine and Mr. Moody, and we sat in the front row.

I don't remember what team Freedom was playing that night, but I know I'll never forget anything else about that game. Miss Delphine had brought her green-and-white pom-poms, and me and her screamed and hollered till our throats hurt. Ray pumped his fist in the air and high-fived me every time Harlem tossed the ball clear across the gym and right into the net. And Mr. Moody? He didn't say much, but his wrinkled, whiskery face looked about as happy and proud as anything.

A couple of times Harlem waved at me. I waved back, wishing I had eyes in the back of my head to see the faces of those girls in the bleachers behind me. Somebody made a muddy footprint on my coat, but I didn't even care.

After the game, we all went to get ice cream. Me and Harlem and Ray and Miss Delphine and Mr. Moody. We talked about how good Harlem did and how many points he scored. And then guess what? Miss Delphine showed us her new tattoo! A tiny little red rose on her ankle.

I ate my chocolate chip ice cream and thought about how everything had turned out so good. I thought about the spelling bee and my backup plan and that day I had left Harlem and Mr. Moody sitting on that cushion in the alley. I watched Harlem jabbering away, sitting up straight and tall with his glasses on. And then I started thinking maybe I really *had* found fame and glory in Freedom, Georgia, after all. Of course, nobody would know it but me and my four friends, but maybe I had found it all the same.

I reckon I'll never get to Disney World, though. But then again, you never know.